SIHA TOOSKIN KNOWS

The Catcher of Dreams

By Charlene Bearhead and Wilson Bearhead

Illustrated by Chloe Bluebird Mustooch

HIGHWATER
PRESS

Canada Council   Conseil des arts
for the Arts   du Canada

We acknowledge the support of the Canada Council for the Arts.
Nous remercions le Conseil des arts du Canada de son soutien.

HighWater Press gratefully acknowledges the financial support of the Province of Manitoba through the Department of Sport, Culture and Heritage and the Manitoba Book Publishing Tax Credit, and the Government of Canada through the Canada Book Fund (CBF), for our publishing activities.

HighWater Press is an imprint of Portage & Main Press.
Printed and bound in Canada by Friesens
Design by Relish New Brand Experience
Cover Art by Chloe Bluebird Mustooch

Library and Archives Canada Cataloguing in Publication

Title: Siha Tooskin knows the catcher of dreams / by Charlene Bearhead and Wilson Bearhead ; illustrated by Chloe Bluebird Mustooch.
Other titles: Catcher of dreams
Names: Bearhead, Charlene, 1963- author. | Bearhead, Wilson, 1958- author. | Mustooch, Chloe Bluebird, 1991- illustrator.
Identifiers: Canadiana (print) 20190058587 | Canadiana (ebook) 20190058625 | ISBN 9781553798323 (softcover) | ISBN 9781553798057 (PDF) | ISBN 9781553798330 (iPad fixed layout)
Classification: LCC PS8603.E245 S49 2020 | DDC jC813/.6—dc23

23 22 21 20   1 2 3 4 5

HIGHWATER
PRESS

www.highwaterpress.com
Winnipeg, Manitoba
Treaty 1 Territory and homeland of the Métis Nation

I dedicate Siha Tooskin Knows the Catcher of Dreams *to the fulfillment of my dreams: my daughter Seneca. Your strength, beauty, and generosity of spirit inspire me each day as I witness you sharing the gifts that have been given to you by so many wonderful people around you.*

—CHARLENE BEARHEAD

We dedicate the Siha Tooskin Knows series to the storytellers who taught us. To those who guided us and shared their knowledge so that we might pass along what we have learned from them to teach children. Their stories are a gentle way of guiding us all along the journey of life.

In that way we tell these stories for our children and grandchildren, and for all children. May they guide you in the way that we have been guided as these stories become part of your story.

—CHARLENE BEARHEAD AND WILSON BEARHEAD

Watch for this little plant!
It will grow as you read, and if you need a break,
it marks a good spot for a rest.

Like a flash of lightning Paul Wahasaypa zipped up the sidewalk and onto the lawn. He jumped off of the blue peddle bike that he was riding and began sprinting towards the front door of his house.

As he dashed past the hedge that separated his family's yard from the one next door, Paul's hand shot up into the air and waved to his new neighbour, Mrs. Carter. She was out checking her mailbox when Paul arrived home. Paul's dad always joked that even though the mail carrier came at the same time every day, Mrs. Carter checked her mailbox at least ten times a day so she could see what everyone in the neighbourhood was doing. Today she lingered an extra-long time at the mailbox as she watched Paul dart across the grass like a starved wolf chasing the last deer on the plains. Mrs. Carter was actually worried and wondered if everything was okay with Paul. She had never seen him racing towards his house like that and she hoped that no one was sick or hurt. For a brief moment she did take a quick glance down the street in case there was actually a starved wolf or coyote chasing Paul. That's when she realized what the emergency was. Paul wasn't

running away from a ravenous grizzly bear and he hadn't seen Shee-ah. Paul was running *towards* his house because he was excited.

As Mrs. Carter scanned the street for clues to solve this great mystery she noticed a light green pickup truck parked in front of Paul's house. Just then she remembered having seen two Elders getting out of that truck when she was out checking her mailbox an hour earlier. They had walked towards the

Wahasaypa home. As she thought back through all of her mailbox checks over the past few months, Mrs. Carter could only recall seeing this truck park on her street once or twice. Now she knew why Paul was in such a rush to get home. His Mitoshin and Mugoshin had come to visit. This must be a very special occasion. Mrs. Carter decided then and there that she would need to check the mailbox a few extra times today, so that she could find out exactly what the big deal was.

"Hi," panted Paul as he stood in the doorway. He was grinning from ear to ear but really out of breath.

"Mitowjin," acknowledged Mugoshin as she looked up from her work with a gentle smile. "How are you doing, my boy?"

"Good," answered Paul. He was still a little out of breath and leaning against the doorway. "Where's Mitoshin?"

"Oh, he went to get your little brother," Mugoshin explained. She set her work down in

her lap and reached out to her grandson to motion that she wanted to give him a hug. "Auntie Robin took Danny home with her this morning so she could watch him until we got here."

By now Paul's energy had returned. He kicked off his shoes and rushed over to hug his Mugoshin.

"You ran all the way home?" she asked her grandson as she put her hands gently on his cheeks. "You've run so fast that you overheated."

"I rode my bike," answered Paul. "Mitoshin always tells me that I need to be aware of my surroundings if I'm going to be a good hunter, so I have to practise even when I'm in town. I was scanning the horizon from the top of the hill eight blocks away and I spotted a green speck that was out of place. Mitoshin always reminds me that we have to train our minds to watch for signs of changes in our environment. I had to dig back quite

a ways through my highly-trained mind," Paul joked. "Of course, I knew in an instant that the green dot that I spotted from the end of the street was your truck, so I rode as fast as I could, zigging and zagging to avoid any possible danger along the way. At one point I'm pretty sure I passed a seagull in mid-flight, I was going so fast. I didn't know you were coming to visit today, so I had to get here as fast as possible to find out what was happening."

"I see that Mitoshin must also be teaching you some of his storytelling skills, Mitowjin," Mugoshin laughed. "The story of your trip home sounds almost as exaggerated as some of Mitoshin's hunting stories."

"We didn't know that we would be visiting today either, but your mom phoned us early this morning to ask us to come," Mugoshin explained. "The new baby is ready to meet the family so your dad took your mom to the hospital." Mugoshin smiled to herself as she picked up her project and started to work on it again. Everyone who knew Mugoshin knew that her grandchildren were the joy of her life. Paul was her first grandchild, and Mitoshin always teased her that she had been so anxious to have a grandchild she had made his moss bag three years before he was even born. Mugoshin thought back to how happy she had been when Danny was born because she had a new baby to rock while she told stories and sang to Paul. Mugoshin was so pleased that she

would have another grandchild soon. The new baby would be a gift no matter what, although Mugoshin wondered if maybe this time she would have a little granddaughter to pass along some of her other teachings to.

Paul's eyes lit up. He smiled to himself as he walked to the kitchen where he could smell the fresh bannock waiting for him. It seemed like he had been waiting forever for the new baby to arrive. Now the baby would finally be here. Paul hadn't said anything, but he secretly hoped that it would be a girl. Just think, his little sister might inherit Mugoshin's great bannock-making skills. She could make bannock every day while Ena was at work.

Maybe she would be really good at beading. If so, Paul could convince her to do some extra beading for his Grass Dance outfit and in exchange, he would trap some weasels for her to make braid extensions for her Jingle Dress outfit...because of course she would be a fantastic Jingle Dress dancer. Yes, Paul figured it would be awesome to have a little sister because he already had a brother.

Paul's mind was filled with so many hopeful thoughts. What if his little sister became the first Nakota woman to rule on a Supreme Court case? What if it was a case designating sacred sites of the First Nations as protected heritage sites completely under the control of the Nation? That would be really cool too. As he sat on the

stool at the kitchen counter and reached for a piece of delicious bannock from the big bowl that Mugoshin had left out for him, his mind continued to wander. He wondered if Supreme Court judges made their own bannock. He knew that if he had a little sister, she would be able to do anything.

Look at Mugoshin and Ena, he thought. They are both busy all the time and they still enjoy making bannock. Mugoshin was so busy with all of the things that she had to take care of, but she knew how much Paul loved her bannock, so she always made it for him when she came to visit.

"This is a great day," Paul thought to himself as he bit into his second piece of bannock. "A new baby, a visit from Mitoshin and Mugoshin, and fresh bannock all on the same day." He carried his tasty snack into the living room and sat down on the couch near Mugoshin.

"Wow, that is beautiful, Mugoshin," Paul said with admiration. "You know, Ena still hangs my dream catcher up above where my head rests each time we move my bed. Danny's too. Both of our dream catchers are beautiful but I've never seen you make one with white plumes before."

"This is a dream catcher I'm going to hang over the new baby's cradle. I did that when you were born and when your brother was born." Mugoshin spoke as she continued to wrap the sinew around the small willow hoop. She began to tell Paul the story of the dream catcher. It was the same story that she told him each time she made a dream catcher for one of her grandchildren. Paul knew the story, but he was always happy to hear it over and over again. It was a good one. Besides, the bowl of bannock was a big one. The longer the story, the bigger the snack.

"Long ago," Mugoshin began, "our families lived together on the land. We would move across the land and live wherever the buffalo led us. Our children could play and move freely in our villages. Our children have always been so precious to us and everyone watched over them while they played. Even at night we had a way to protect our children as we slept and as they slept."

"Our mothers and grandmothers would call upon the grandmother and grandfather spirits to protect us while we were sleeping. They would smudge with sweetgrass or sage and ask the Creator to keep us safe. At some point along the way we started to hang dream catchers like this one above the heads of our babies and children as they slept."

"We offer tobacco and choose a willow branch to make the circle of life. It's the circle of our families and communities that keeps our children safe and protected. Inside the circle of life is a web of support for the child. The web is woven from sinew that is strong and unbreakable like the bond between our families and our children."

"We place a small stone on one of the strands of the web. This stone reminds us to always stay close to our mother: Ena Makoochay. She is the one who teaches all of us how to be mothers, and how to feed and provide for our children."

"Once the dream catcher is finished, we smudge it and ask for blessings on our child, asking that the power of good spirits and positive energy protect the child."

"At night when a child is sleeping, dreams come. Every dream must pass through the dream catcher to get to the child. The power of the smudge and prayers ensures that the good dreams pass right through the web of the dream catcher and slide gently down the feather that hangs from the bottom of the willow hoop. They drift down onto the sleepy little one and bring peaceful rest."

"When we smudge the dream catcher, we are asking for the bad dreams to be trapped in the small holes of the web where they are kept away from the sleeping child. In the first morning light, the bad dreams vanish as the sunlight hits them." Mugoshin looked up at her grandson to be sure that he was hearing this important part of her teaching. "You see, Siha Tooskin, evil cannot live in the light of truth. The light that comes from grandfather sun exposes all things for what they really are. We can see things clearly in the light of day where nothing can hide. In this way the bad dreams can be seen for what they really are. They disappear to avoid being found out."

Mugoshin affirmed her teaching with a gentle nod towards her grandson and then in the direction of the work she held in her hands. "And that is how the dream catcher protects our precious children from bad dreams, Siha Tooskin."

Paul knew what Mugoshin meant about evil not being able to live in the light of truth. He thought about the stories that Ade and Ena would tell about the churches taking their cousins and forcing them into residential schools. Paul remembered his friend Jeff's parents being shocked when they learned that Paul's grandparents had not been allowed to vote until 1960 simply because they were First Nation.

Even Paul's teacher, Ms. Baxter, hadn't known about the Pass System until after the Truth and Reconciliation Commission of Canada happened and teachers started to learn the true history of Canada, including the experiences of Indigenous people.

Ms. Baxter tells the class that the truth is only now being taught and it is shedding light on the horrors of our history in Canada. She says that we must all strive to ensure that human rights violations against Indigenous people don't continue now that everyone knows the truth.

In Paul's mind shedding the light of truth was like the sunlight in the story of the dream catcher: they both stop bad things from happening.

By the time that Mugoshin had finished her story, she had finished weaving the web inside the willow hoop of the dream catcher and Paul had finished his bannock. Mugoshin turned to Paul and raised the circular web for him to hold. While Paul held it firmly Mugoshin tied the soft, white plume to the bottom of the hoop. Paul had a good feeling about this, knowing that eagle plumes are sacred. He had been taught that they carry our words straight to the Creator because the eagle flies higher than any other bird. Knowing this, Paul wished extra hard for a little sister while he held the willow hoop for Mugoshin.

"There," said Mugoshin as she took the finished dream catcher back from Paul. "Now we're ready for the new baby."

Just then Paul heard the back door open and the phone ring all at the same time. Paul turned towards the kitchen. Through the doorway he saw Mitoshin pick up the phone receiver with one hand and wave to Paul with the other.

At that instant, Paul's little brother Danny came running across the living room, climbed up on Mugoshin's lap, and threw his little arms around her neck for a hug.

Paul barely even noticed Danny because he was so busy trying to hear what Mitoshin was talking about on the phone. Paul couldn't hear what Mitoshin was saying, but judging by the smile on his face Paul was pretty sure that it must be Ade on the other end of that conversation.

After a minute or two Mitoshin hung up the phone. He walked into the living room and looked at Paul with a smile. "What are you waiting for, Siha Tooskin?" he asked. "You should be putting on your shoes. We have to go to the hospital to meet your baby sister."

"All right!!!" Paul exclaimed as he jumped off the couch and onto his feet. "Can I call Uncle Lenard first to tell him we have a new Jingle Dress dancer in our family?"

"Okay," Mitoshin replied, "but make it quick and tell him to meet us at the hospital. Your mom really wants to see you, and I know how long you two old men can stay on the phone when you start talking about powwow."

"I'll make it fast," Paul promised as he picked up the phone to call Uncle Lenard. Paul tried to be cool, but he could hardly contain his excitement. He finally had a little sister. The women's teachings from Ena and Mugoshin would live on in his family now for sure.

Glossary

Ade	Dad or father
Ena	Mom or mother
Ena Makoochay	Mother Earth
Mitoshin	Grandfather
Mitowjin	My grandchild
Mugoshin	Grandmother
Shee-ah	Monster
Siha Tooskin	Little Foot (siha is foot; tooskin is little)
Wayasaypa	Bear head

A note on use of the Nakota language in this book series from Wilson Bearhead:

The Nakota dialect used in this series is the Nakota language as taught to Wilson by his grandmother, Annie Bearhead, and used in Wabamun Lake First Nation. Wilson and Charlene have chosen to spell the Nakota words in this series phonetically as Nakota was never a written language. Any form of written Nakota language that currently exists has been developed in conjunction with linguists who use a Eurocentric construct.

ABOUT THE AUTHORS

Charlene Bearhead is an educator and Indigenous education advocate. She was the first Education Lead for the National Centre for Truth and Reconciliation and the Education Coordinator for the National Inquiry into Missing and Murdered Indigenous Women and Girls. Charlene was recently honoured with the Alumni Award from the University of Alberta and currently serves as the Director of Reconciliation for *Canadian Geographic*. She is a mother and a grandmother who began writing stories to teach her own children as she raised them. Charlene lives near Edmonton, Alberta with her husband Wilson.

Wilson Bearhead, a Nakota Elder and Wabamun Lake First Nation community member in central Alberta (Treaty 6 territory), is the recent recipient of the Canadian Teachers' Federation Indigenous Elder Award. Currently, he is the Elder for Elk Island Public Schools. Wilson's grandmother Annie was a powerful, positive influence in his young life, teaching him all of the lessons that gave him the strength, knowledge, and skills to overcome difficult times and embrace the gifts of life.

ABOUT THE ILLUSTRATOR

Chloe Bluebird Mustooch is from the Alexis Nakoda Sioux Nation of central Alberta, and is a recent graduate of the Emily Carr University of Art + Design. She is a seamstress, beadworker, illustrator, painter, and sculptor. She was raised on the reservation, and was immersed in hunting, gathering, and traditional rituals, and she has also lived in Santa Fe, New Mexico, an area rich in art and urbanity.